cinderella
jumproperhymes

CINDERELLA JUMP ROPE RHYMES
A CABINET DES FÉES PRODUCTION
www.cabinetdesfees.com
Copyright © 2012 Cabinet des Fées
Images © Adam Oehlers
Rhymes © Individual Authors
Introduction © Francesca Forrest
All Rights Reserved Worldwide
Published by Papaveria Press
(an imprint of Circle Six)
in Great Britain

With special thanks
to Francesca Forrest
for curating and editing the rhymes.

ISBN 978-1-907881-16-9

CONTRIBUTORS:

Sonya Taaffe
Francesca Forrest
Samantha Henderson
Erik Amundsen
Rose Lemberg
Nadia Bulkin
Julia Rios
Kyle Davis

PAPAVERIA PRESS

www.papaveria.com

> Cinderella, dressed in yella
> Went downstairs to kiss her fella
> By mistake she kissed a snake
> How many doctors did it take?
> *One, Two, Three, Four...*

This jump rope rhyme was in actual use in the United States at least as late as the 1970s and 1980s. I can remember jumping rope to it, or this variant:

> Cinderella, dressed in yella,
> Went downstairs to kiss her fella
> By mistake her girdle busted
> How many people were disgusted?
> *One, Two, Three, Four...*

Fast forward to nowadays, and put that rhyme in the hands of speculative poets and short-story writers and their friends. These are people with a lurid sense of humor, a color palette not limited to yellow, and a deep interest in imagining for Cindy some life-changing experiences beyond snake kissing and girdle busting.

Erik Amundsen kicked off the freestyling on his Livejournal in 2010. More and more people stopped by to add rhymes, and in the end there were contributions from Nadia Bulkin, Kyle Davis, myself, Samantha Henderson, Rose Lemberg, Julia Rios, and Sonya Taaffe. We thought the rhymes were too fun not to share with a broader audience, and fortunately, the inestimable Ezebet YellowBoy of Papaveria Press agreed. We enlisted the brilliant illustrator Adam Oehlers to help with the project, and you see before you the final result. We hope you enjoy it! All proceeds will be used to support *Cabinet des Fées* and charities of its choice.

—Francesca Forrest

Cinderella, dressed in red
ate Snow White's apple
now she's dead!

Cinderella dressed in scarlet

went downtown

to beat a harlot

used a fence post as a truncheon

and beat her from the morn to luncheon.

Cinderella dressed in white

stared at the sun

and lost her sight

her eyeballs burned to little cinders

still hot enough to cook your dinner.

Cinderella dressed in violet

got a note

from Pontius Pilate.

 dressed in indigo

flew to the moon

on a pink flamindigo.

Cinderella dressed in black...

killed all the robots
WITH HER BLAST ATTACK.

Cinderella dressed in jade
stole her love's heart, knived and flayed,
held it up against the sun,
dressed in gold, the final one.

Cinderella dressed in grey
had the face of a jaguar
and a sailor's sway
beaten clean between two stones
her children shined like polished bones.

Cinderella, in panther skin
Frightened her lover with a sharp-toothed grin
He tried to flee, but she was too fast
And she made of him a fine repast.

Cinderella dressed in puce
picked oranges to make some juice
spilled the pulp upon her shoe
decided she would eat a gnu.

Cinderella, dressed in orange
recommended eating borage.

Cinderella, dressed in teal,
put some borage on the grill.

Cinderella, dressed in gray,
claimed that borage was passé.

Cinderella, dressed in borage,
checked all poets into storage.

Cinderella, dressed in orange
went to Lowes to get a door-hinge!

Cinderella, dressed in pink
met a ghost
and made it blink.

Cinderella, dressed in turquoise
woke up late
to an awful noise
rolled right over on her cat
and nearly squashed the poor thing flat!

Cinderella dressed in green
nah, that's too easy
let's be mean!

Cinderella dressed in green
Lost eighty years in her time machine.
Dressed in black crape, dressed in earth,
she was buried before her birth.

Cinderella dressed in rust
shook off the years
and rose from her dust
made of ash and made of smoke
she searches the land
for a prince to choke.

Cinderella, in vermillion
danced all night at the cotillion
lost her virtue in a drinking game
came home happy all the same.

Cinderella dressed in purple
looked for deep ones
that could burble
found that Dagon's breath was bad
and told him things that drove him mad!

Cinderella got undressed
paid for some augmented breasts
with make-up like a drunken whore
she joined the cast of Jersey Shore.

Cinderella dressed in flame
lives up to the mythic name
people think she's just coquettish
but it's really a shoe fetish.

Cinderella, dressed in nubuck,
went to exorcise her dybbuk.
Unfortunately, a full rabbinic session
proved much worse than demonic possession.

Cinderella dressed in puce,
Liked to date Hasidic Jews.
it's how her fancy gets its tickles,
by enjoying kosher pickles.

Cinderella wearing lemon
lent her laptop to a gremlin
hope her hard drive was external,
a gremlin virus is eternal.

Cinderella wearing lime
got involved with corporate crime
her finances aren't all they seem,
since she runs a Ponzi scheme
don't expect her to amend
until she's facing five to ten.

Cinderella dressed in aqua

felt she had unbalanced chakras,

ran into some Tibetan monks

and got the Dalai Lama drunk.

Once they were all good and hammered,

A policeman put them in the slammer.

Cindy couldn't post her bail,

So she sent some chain e-mail.

How many forwards did it take...?

ARTIST

ADAM OEHLERS was born in Coventry, raised in Ireland and then Australia and is now back in the UK working out of Brighton. His illustration work has been exhibited worldwide and has been published in books for both adults and children. His publications include *A Babble of Words*, *The Rhyme of the Ancient Mariner*, *Celeste*, *Nick and the Magical Tea Party* and *Dear Little Emmie*. Examples of his work and publications can be found on his website at www.adamoehlers.com.

ARTIST STATEMENT:
"I like to think that all of my images and sculptures belong to the same little universe, built by the stories of each of the characters that inhabit it. It is a world that is not so different from ours, a grim, cobbled place that is trapped in its own time, with some little elements of odd magic which creep in at the edges."

CONTRIBUTORS

FRANCESCA FORREST highly approves of the broadest possible array of colors, jump rope rhymes, and Cinderella, and is happy to be among the contributors to this little book.

ERIK AMUNDSEN was removed from display as he was considered zoologically improbable and/or terrifying to small children.

NADIA BULKIN writes and studies international politics at American University. She's from Jakarta, Indonesia, by way of Lincoln, Nebraska. Most of the time, she writes "horror stories about the self."

KYLE DAVIS is a personal trainer and yoga instructor and massage therapist living in Seattle, Washington, who thinks cooking, running and being witty are man's greatest natual talents, and is constantly wishing he was more talented.

SAMANTHA HENDERSON lives in Covina, California, by way of England, South Africa, Illinois and Oregon. Her short fiction and poetry have been published in *Realms of Fantasy*, *Strange Horizons*, *Goblin Fruit*, *Weird Tales*, and reprinted in *The Year's Best Fantasy and Science Fiction*, *Steampunk II: Steampunk Reloaded*, and is upcoming in *The Mammoth Book of Steampunk*. She is the co-winner of the 2010 Rhysling Award for speculative poetry and is the author of the Forgotten Realms novel *Dawnbringer*. For more information, please see her website at www.samanthahenderson.com.

ROSE LEMBERG is an immigrant from three countries. In her copious spare time, Rose plucks poems from slush, writes about imaginary people, and waits for her treen eggs to hatch. She exorcises her dybbuks regularly to no observable effect. For more, visit http://roselemberg.net.

JULIA RIOS writes speculative prose and poetry. She's also the staff interviewer for *Stone Telling* and hosts the Outer Alliance Podcast (celebrating LGBTQIA content in speculative fiction). She's half-Mexican, but her (fairly dreadful) French is better than her Spanish. She has blue hair and brown eyes, though these things are subject to change without notice. Visit her online at http://www.juliarios.com.

SONYA TAAFFE's published work includes the collections *Singing Innocence and Experience* and *Postcards from the Province of Hyphens* and the Rhysling-winning poem "Matlacihuatl's Gift." She holds master's degrees in Classics from Brandeis and Yale and once named a Kuiper belt object. She would add that she is the real-life original of a character by Neal Stephenson, but as said character is five years old and spends most of their screentime drinking cranberry juice, this is a somewhat less badass achievement than it sounds.

CPSIA information can be obtained
at www.ICGtesting.com
Printed in the USA
LVIC041534180412
278100LV00001B